Anne Wilsdorf
PHILOMENE

Greenwillow Books

NEW YORK

FOR BERIVAN AND MENELIK AND THÉODORE
AND ARMELLE AND DAMARIS AND GWENAËLLE
AND JULIEN AND PILI AND POLO

Library of Congress Cataloging-in-Publication Data
Wilsdorf, Anne.
Philomene / Anne Wilsdorf.
p.   cm.
Translation of: Philomène.
Summary: Plucky Philomene turns the tables on a
nasty witch by befriending her pet monster.
ISBN 0-688-10369-3. ISBN 0-688-10370-7 (lib. bdg.)
[1. Witches—Fiction.   2. Monsters—Fiction.]   I. Title.
PZ7.W6858Ph   1992   [E]—dc20   90-24295   CIP   AC

A witch lived in the deepest part of the forest.
That's what the children said. They even claimed
that anyone who went near her would immediately
be turned into a frog. Everyone believed the story,
everyone . . . except Philomene.
"I'll go into the forest by myself and prove your silly
witch doesn't exist," she announced. "Then we'll
be able to play wherever we like."

Philomene grabbed her little
red pocketbook and set off.
"See you later," she called.

She walked and walked until she came to a spot where
the trees seemed the most monstrous and threatening.
There she stopped and called, "OLD WITCH, FLEA OF THE
FOREST, COME ON OUT IF YOU ARE REAL. HERE I AM!"

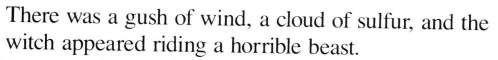

There was a gush of wind, a cloud of sulfur, and the witch appeared riding a horrible beast.

"Hee, hee, hee," she cackled. "So you are the insolent wench who has come to trouble my peace? You shall be punished for this!"

Philomene felt the claws of the monster
as he lifted her up.
"To the castle!" ordered the witch.

"What an ugly place this is," said Philomene. "And it's dirty, too."

"Well, then, you can make it sparkle. That's a good job for you, little girl," said the witch, and she handed Philomene a bucket and broom. "I'll give you until tonight, and you'll be sorry if the job isn't well done!"

"That's exactly what I think," said Philomene with a glint in her eye.

Philomene scrubbed and
cleaned, scrubbed and cleaned
till at the end of the day
the floor shone
like a mirror...

and was as slippery as a skating rink.
WHAM! The monster, who had come with
the witch to inspect Philomene's work,
fell flat on his back, unconscious.

"You dare laugh, little pest? Just wait!" the witch
hissed furiously. After carrying the monster to
his room, she grabbed Philomene by the ear and
threw her in with him.

"When he comes to, he will finish you off for a snack,"
the witch said spitefully.

Philomene landed at the monster's feet.
She looked up at him. He didn't seem all
that terrible. He had a bump on his head,
his right paw was a little bent, and his
left wing was slightly torn.

Philomene began to feel sorry for him. She
got some ointment and bandages out of her
little red pocketbook and went to work.
Just then the monster woke up and
grabbed Philomene...

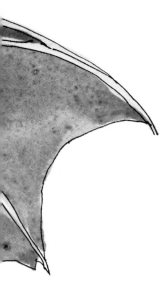

and gave her a kiss.
They were friends.

Suddenly they heard the witch's
footsteps in the distance.
Philomene took a chicken bone
out of her pocketbook and
threw it on the ground.
Then she climbed into the
monster's ear to hide.

The witch cackled with glee when she saw
the small bone.
"Hee, hee, hee. Here's all that's left of that
impudent little thing."

That night, when the witch was asleep,
Philomene and the monster went to the
witch's laboratory. They mixed up all
her potions, lotions, and broths, and
rewrote her evil spells.

In the morning everything went wrong for the witch.

Her broom started doing loops
in the air.

No matter how tightly she held on,
no matter how loudly she recited
all her magical spells, she
couldn't keep from falling...

straight down the chimney of her own castle.
She landed at the feet of Philomene and the monster.

"This time I'll get you!" screamed the witch.
She pointed the remains of her magic wand at
the little girl and uttered the terrible words
that change children into frogs:
"ABRI ABRA CADABRA FROGIE FROGA GRODADA..."

But what happened?
It was the wicked witch
who turned into a frog.

Philomene climbed on the monster's back, and they
flew away from the castle. The monster landed
gently at the edge of the woods.
"Will we see each other again soon?" he asked.
"Of course!" promised Philomene.

"Philomene is back!" her friends cried happily.
"She was right! There is no witch!"
And they all went off together to play in the forest.